GW01086511

THE TWO NEROS

Peter Cordwell

For Agnes
and her great staff
at Chislehurst

up anywhere near my usual table – smile, wave or thumbs up – I can keep myself mostly to myself. That's down to the coffee, flat white extra hot; a chicken and bacon toastie or apricot croissant; my latest Rex Stout/Nero Wolfe mystery; and perhaps most of all the music, mainly cool jazzy stuff on incredibly well-chosen loops.

So that's where and how I got to know Georgia, and no, I didn't make the first move. I'd noticed her before, of course, in one of her green tops and mass of tangled red hair, and the laptop she carried to one of the five tables at the far end, where students and various individuals 'working from home' have their backs to the wall.

That particularly busy morning Georgia was making her way down the aisle when her progress was halted by a lumbering labradoodle on its way out of the dog-friendly coffee shop. It gave her the chance to glance across and ask: 'Good book? You're always reading in here.' I said great book, showing her the cover – The Doorbell Rang by Rex Stout – and added: 'Much better than reading phones.'

She smiled and – surprisingly – sat right down, placing her laptop on my small round table as the labradoodle looked on. 'This okay?' she asked, meaning sitting there. 'I just love talking about authors and books. Words are wonderful, aren't they? Actually, it's my work as well.'

'Really?' I said, entering into the spirit of things and realising Georgia might be one of those characters who capture what seems like five years inside five minutes. 'What kind of work?'

'Freelance proof reading mainly,' she said, talking quickly. 'I also try to write a bit myself. I joined an amateur drama group in Eltham and I'm so excited they're working on something I've written, a shortish comedy drama called Dictaphone. It's about...sorry, I'm carrying on again. (Exactly as I would.) Why don't we just get going like we usually do and chat a bit later? I've got a bit of work to finish off and you obviously love your Rex Stout...it's so nice to talk to you at last.'

I said that was a good idea, getting back into Archie Goodwin's narration, Wolfe in this particular story taking on J. Edgar Hoover and the FBI in brilliant and hilarious fashion at the brownstone, 922 West 35th Street. Georgia's top matched her eyes – more bluey-green than blue - and it must have been all of 10 minutes later that she plonked down the laptop lid and said: 'Right, Rex Stout, what a name, tell me all about him, if you don't mind. I've never read any of his stuff. I haven't even heard of him.'

I still had half a page of Chapter 7 to finish but gladly answered the call. 'Well,' I said, matching her enthusiasm, 'he writes about a genius overweight private detective in New York called Nero Wolfe and his gallivanting young assistant Archie Goodwin, who narrates all the novels and novellas, must be over 70 of them, and does all the running around. And the amazing thing is that Stout – born in Noblesville, Indiana, in 1886 - didn't start writing about Wolfe until his late forties. He'd been a child maths prodigy who went on to make a mint showing literally hundreds of schools and colleges across America how to run their banking systems, whatever that entailed. He died, aged 88, in 1975, his later stuff as fresh as you like.'

I put the brakes on. I also didn't want to 'carry on' in the way that irritates some people I know, but just had to add: 'Plus... plus, Rex Todhunter Stout was also a good lad in everyday life. How about this, he actually led the So-

ciety for the prevention of World War Three…'
I paused again, thinking it wise, then: 'Oh, and
he's got a really neat way of recommending
books by other writers. Archie's narrations in-
variably include Wolfe dog-earing pages of his
own latest book in the brownstone, I Googled
Beauty for Ashes by Christopher La Farge,
whoever he was. Hardcover £210.80p on Amazon! And it's a novel in verse! I don't think I
could take that…'

'Me neither,' said Georgia. 'Poems for po-
etry, in my opinion. Do not go gentle…'

'Exactly,' said I, wondering whether to tell
her I banged out the odd short story myself
and had had some published on Amazon,
where else, and being all of 56 quid up. I de-
cided not to. I could save all that. Instead, I
asked Georgia to tell me more about the proof
reading. I'm glad I did because it soon became
very much Mr Amateur meets little Miss Professional.

She rattled on entertainingly through spell-
ing, grammar, text flow, continuity, motiva-
tion, dialogue – I'll show her this one, one day
– plans, outlines and brainstorms…self-pub-
lishing and, of course, writer's block.

I added a modest nod to what I hope

looked like an intelligent expression, and said: 'Ah, and how long have you been doing it, this proof reading lark, young Georgia?' We'd exchanged names soon after the labradoodle had got bored and left. She said four or five years but hoped that the writing would take over completely before she reached 35, at which point we were able to admit to being 33 and 41.

Having done Stout to death, I asked her about the authors she liked most and maybe one or two she didn't. Myself, for example, I've always had this thing about George Orwell fighting at the front in Spain and getting shot in the neck while Hemingway booked in a bit on the side at the nearest Premier Inn.

Georgia had a lovely way of building herself up to a telling contribution, moving her bottom about until she was properly comfortable, jogging her arms and top half an inch or two in different directions, and looking you dead in the eye, not unlike how I imagine Dolly Parton would be, or Gordon Banks preparing to save a penalty.

'The first female author that comes to mind is Jane Austen,' said Georgia, 'and how her female protagonists were way ahead of their time. They're highly intellectual, with Austen emphasising the need for a good education... not just the traditional academic education, but learning about self-independence, self-esteem, self-improvement etc, and focusing on moral development – it's like Austen was a self-development guru before her time! I love that about her characters.'

I almost said I intended to read Emma, reckoned by some to be Austen's best book, but I just 'Hmmed' and asked Georgia who she did the proof reading for. 'Mainly for a very bright young woman called Jessica Grace Coleman. Look her up. I've learned so much from her, the importance and power of words, and how the words we use – about others, about ourselves – matter, even if we don't realise it, whether in a book or in life itself.

'It's the kind of work where you find it difficult to turn off your proof-reading brain, even in daily life where you see incorrect apostrophes on signage or in people's emails. This happens with every proof reader I know, along with discussing The Oxford Commas...and semi-colons, of course.'

I'd have to get used to all that if this developed, and learn something from it, and maybe come back with a point or two myself to keep up. See if she agreed, for example, with the importance of a twist in a short story. Did Dictaphone, for example, have a twist to it? I was told that it most definitely did!

The chatting got easier and slightly less intense as we both began to relax with each other. It was obvious that overdoing it could be a problem, especially for me, so I made a point of cutting my contributions by about a fifth. I don't think she ever did; she didn't need to; women don't need to, do they, generally?

One factual thing that did surprise me was how much ghost-writing and editing Georgia did on older people's memoirs and life stories, their autobiographies in fact. Not Arsenal players or astronauts, just ordinary folk: 'I get a lot of these – mostly about how important they think it is to get their stories down on paper for future generations of their family to read and learn from.'

That one threw me a bit, probably because I couldn't imagine doing it myself, but Georgia's enthusiasm brought on another 'Hmm' and encouraged me to cast a glance at the managing barista whose own unbounded enthusiasm, amid all the hurry-scurry, was another thing that made this Nero so special. I'd certainly like to read her life story. Previously and somewhat sneakily, I'd found out that she was Hungarian with a name that I saw only as old English. Agnes! You could tell every time you went there that Agnes's own moral development was all that it needed to be, and some.

Georgia had to go but not before saying that we had to chat again over coffee and croissants. 'The best times for me,' she said, forthright as ever, 'are Friday and Monday mornings, around half-ten to eleven.' I said that was exactly the same for me, without going off into the wonders of synchronicity. That would take a whole session and might even lead to Bashar, the extra-terrestrial from light years away being 'channelled' on YouTube.

This was a Friday and I knew I'd be there on Monday at 10.30 with Nero in Nero. As she left, she said: 'What do you do, by the way?' I said I'd tell her next time. She got to the door, turned her red head, smiled and waved goodbye. She looked again through the big window by the door. Agnes looked over at me at the same time and smiled her smile as well.

I was there on the Monday, but no Georgia, which was fine in the overall scheme of things.

I sat there thinking how much this particular Caffè Nero must have been home or harbour to bright new friendships, and how important something like that was. There had been one or two pubs down the years that had played similar roles for me, the late, lamented Director General in Woolwich and the old style Dacre Arms in Lee springing to mind, but this coffee place 'took the giddy biscuit', as P.G. Wodehouse, a good friend of Stout's, put it in one of his own stories.

Georgia was there first on the Friday, sitting at the back with her laptop and latte. She motioned to the other seat at her table as mine. I gave her the thumbs up as I waited for my usual tray and the loyalty stamp. When I joined her I asked her if she wanted anything to nibble; it wouldn't take a moment, recommending the vegan sausage roll; but she declined before doing what she does best, taking over, which was fine with me.

'Right,' she said, 'I'd like to suggest the same configuration as last Friday. I've got longer this time, about an hour, but I need to work away for a good few minutes. It's the way I am. Is that okay with you, young Roger?'

'Perfectly,' I said. 'The flat white's extra hot

and Archie's in full flow. J. Edgar...'

She interrupted: 'Just one thing that's been on my mind all week. So what exactly do you do?'

'Well,' I said, 'I've been a bit similar to you as it happens, a journo, a few Fleet Street shifts down the years but mainly local rags. I like meeting people, local people, their lives and joys and troubles, not making stuff up for a Maxwell or a Murdoch.'

She tried to interrupt again but I interrupted her interruption, needing to get this one straight: 'I still do some freelance work and get a call for the odd journalistic project or two, but my main job, if you can call it a job, is something I set up myself a while ago.

'I run a thing online called The Placepotters.'

Georgia: 'The what?'

'Placepotters.'

It was fun to see her thrown for once, and, instead of just asking me to explain, she tried to put it in words herself like a proof reader would: 'You place potters in places where they're wanted or needed? Potters in businesses or in schools and colleges? Or evening classes? I've heard of the London Potters, and I've heard of Potters resorts. They're in Norfolk. I went there once as a kid....'

'No,' I said calmly. 'Horse racing.'

She pulled a face that people like Georgia don't really like to pull, one that shows an unexpected existential threat to the power and understanding of words, so it was time to let her off the hook and explain in time-honoured fashion: 'Sorry, Georgia, I'll make it as clear as I can. What it is, a Placepot is a popular horse racing bet where you have to get a horse, or more than one horse, placed in the first six races at a meeting.'

I soon realised that an explanation to someone who's never heard of it, and probably not the least bit interested in it, could make The Trial by Kafka seem like Crossroads in comparison, so I just as quickly speeded it all up by saying that getting a horse placed meant it finishing in the first three in most races, but first or second in races with fewer than eight runners, and in the first four in races with 16 or more runners.

I omitted the fact that the last-named races had to be 'handicaps', thinking it best not to go into the history of handicaps with Georgia. But purely for colour – which I thought she'd appreciate – I said horses are best drawn low at places like Chester and Lingfield, and especially in seven-furlong races at Dunstall Park, otherwise known as Wolverhampton.

By 'drawn' I meant which stalls the horses were given, very much in relation to their chances at the first bend, which at Wolverhampton...

'Yes,' said Georgia, needing to join in, 'but what do you do for the people who become Placepotters?' Avoiding words like naps, bankers, geldings and yankees, I explained that for a fiver every Saturday 'punters' who subscribed had a chance of a big win for a small outlay, the winnings shared by all of us and with five per cent going to The Injured Jockeys Fund. I think I got away with explaining just enough.

I added: 'I choose the number of horses we need per race and the punters take turns in making the selections for all of us. The vast majority follow the action race by race on television, so there's very much an enjoyment factor to it all as well.'

'How many Placepotters are involved?'

'We've been going for just on three years and we've just passed the 500 punters mark, all over the country, from Catford to Carlisle.'

'£2,500 every Saturday?'

'Yes, but just a fiver each, the price of a coffee and a giddy biscuit.'

Suddenly it sounded more exciting than literature, than reading a book to yourself on a bench. I could even sense a small change in Georgia, but I also added: 'Actually, I think it's also very similar to the work you do, Georgia, with people writing their life stories. Communicating with ordinary people, even though there's nothing ordinary about ordinary people, is there? They're all special, aren't they?'

It felt like some kind of equaliser with this special friend of mine, the way we both liked to get involved with people, the way we both took to chatting to people, to each other, in this difficult existence. I added lightly and brightly: 'I also write short stories for fun on Amazon. Must write one about you!'

My flat white was no longer extra hot but, after a short silence, we were back in the configuration, a slightly different Georgia getting her head down to decide on commas or colons, and Archie recounting a hell of a shock for Hoover's team of tough guys in New York City. (I read Nero in Nero's or in bed, so it's always nice and slow and easy going, really enjoyable).

Georgia did ask me about the short stories and I limited my reply to Bumping Into Christopher Hadley, someone from primary school who was very clever, much cleverer than me but nice with it; what an effect he had on me, even though we weren't best friends or anything.

I took a moment to look over the top of my Mass Market Paperback and take in something of the person opposite, working away. Some girl, as Hemingway might have put it in, what was it, To Have and Have Not? There was a zing about Georgia; and loved the hair.

When we did get chatting normally again I suppose the subject was inevitable, and it would be Georgia who brought it up. Women are braver than men, which is why they like to meet and talk in groups while men only sing when they're winning. But it wasn't about gambling or books. She readjusted herself as usual and said: 'So how are we both fixed, Roger? I'm quite recently divorced and don't really want to go into details right now, if you don't mind. What about your good self?'

I told Georgia I was also on my Tod Sloan and didn't see people much, apart from visiting the two local newsrooms with a feature or page lead, or even a match report, and supermarket queues. I didn't want to go into it either, and it obviously suited us both. It was a good, smiley agreement, even with the slightest tinge of embarrassment.

I regained the reins for a moment or two, saying that it had been great to get to the stage of talking like this – delayed intros and syllables being the thing for the two of us in our different ways, and hoping there were many more where they came from.

'Good points, Roger,' she said, getting the point, and zooming off again: 'Did I tell you about Proofed?'

'Proofed?'

'Yes, Proofed. It's the other gang I work for.'

'Oh, proofed. More proof reading.'

'Yes, they started in England but are now registered in the USA – look 'em up - and have 750 editors worldwide, including little old me.'

I got in that I wouldn't want anyone messing about with my stuff, not even her. 'It would take all the fun out of it, Georgia, make it too academic, too stuffy, like they do with Orwell. He went to war, to coal faces with miners, and walked with tramps, but there's one where the writer pontificates how he would have had done things differently in sleepy bloody Southwold!'

Agnes wondered what the noise was about as Georgia said: 'You talk a lot about Orwell.'

'Well, he's worth it, my girl, he's more relevant than ever, and one thing I don't get is the comparison with Huxley. You read every day about something Orwellian but never about anything Huxleyesque. There was a piece in the Financial Times' Saturday section a good while ago pitting one against the other; by half time it was Orwell 6 Huxley nil.'

I must have stuck 'my girl' in automatically; neither of us took it any further, at least not openly.

After a short silence, I asked Georgia to get back to a previous subject, and she proceeded to make a good case for smartening up the presentation of people's life stories for grandkids to read, and we ended up touching fists to signal a draw. Nice knuckles. At the same time I had been wondering about the results of her divorce and my own mid-life skirmishes. Outside of Nero's it might have taken a turn for better or worse, but inside it was still more or less a non-starter.

Typically, it was Georgia who went off on

another tangent. 'I really like Emily Bronte,' she said. 'She's such a Goth.'

'Wuthering Heights, wasn't it, and that sister of hers wrote Jane Ayre?'

'Charlotte, yes. There was so much death around then... no cure for tuberculosis. It's not surprising they wrote grim stories.'

I added my own doubts about drifting around aimlessly on the moors at the dead of night, and whether I would ever fancy a pint with Heathcliff. I said I probably needed a bit less Wuthering Heights and a bit more Watford.

'Who's your favourite author from that period then?'

'Dickens'll do!' I said out loud 'Prolific, great plots, great characters and great names! And most of all Sydney Carton with two 'y's'! If I could be one person from literature it would probably be Sydney. Or maybe Yossarian.

She saw herself more as Maggie Tulliver in The Mill on the Floss as any thoughts I had of taking this relationship outside of Nero's drifted downstream once again. I didn't know if it was her, me or both of us, probably mainly me. Or maybe mainly her. You can never really tell, can you?

And so it went on, more or less fancy free.

But every time it was great to see Georgia striding into Caffè Nero or me spotting her at the back on her laptop, waving that wave of hers. Mostly on Friday mornings, sometimes Mondays and Fridays, the odd no show from her because of work. Oddly, we didn't ever text. Of course I wondered if she was 'seeing' someone and, since the subject never came up, I assumed she was. I wasn't; I was only seeing her.

I got round to telling her about the other gambling I did, 'professional' because it wasn't tenners or twenties at the local Ladbrokes. It was hundreds or sometimes as much as a thousand. Not my own money, of course, but knowing where to put it on for people with proper dosh, half a dozen of them, having been introduced to it all years earlier by my uncles from 'the Fontwell days', Alan and Tommy.

'Funnily enough, it's all about trust,' I told Georgia. 'As with the Placepotting, the gamblers trust me and when you get a really good tip, often from Ireland, some trainer/owner or other, you have to keep it to yourself and not show off by giving it to friends. Ten per cent if it wins, five if it loses for just getting them on.'

'I could do with a good tip from time to time,' said Georgia, wriggling away, but I quickly suggested we should both be happy as freelances with Friday and Monday mornings to spare, and leave it at that. I added that she wouldn't be seeing me the following week because of Cheltenham.

'Cheltenham?'

'The horse-racing festival. Over the jumps. Every March. I'll be there with Uncle Alan. Planning on Monday and heading west for the rest of the week, staying at a nice little place that he knows. Some people prefer Royal Ascot but Cheltenham is best; none of those silly bloody hats, men's as well as women's. Proletarian, me.'

'Like Winston Smith.'

'Not exactly, but certainly along those lines.'

It was conversations like these that probably defined what some people might call a relationship. We certainly 'dated' virtually every week but never outside the walls of Nero in Chislehurst, not even a suggestion of taking our coffees to watch the ducks in the pond a few yards further up the high street. Theatre, film, meal? No, they never came up. They crossed my mind, of course, but I don't know if they crossed hers. She had to be seeing someone.

You probably think I did, but I didn't mind.

I hate that phrase 'it is what it is,' but maybe it was what it was. Georgia was just great company – we'd never run out of stories or characters or things to talk about, including in our own lives; we were also both a bit Left; up for the underdog – and in the back of my head I thought I would probably use at least some of it in a short story, one day.

One week there was no Georgia on the Friday or the Monday, or the following Friday. On that day Agnes handed me an envelope with what she said was a note 'from your girl… your friend.' She still didn't know our names, and I didn't tell her I knew hers.

It was more a short letter than a note, Georgia saying that her Ex was not well 'in more ways than one,' and how silly we were not to have each other's mobile numbers, if only for texts. She gave me her number but said it was best to text, not call. She was sorry for the melodrama but couldn't really help it.

I texted her and said all was fine and hoped she was okay, and him as well. I didn't know his name and didn't need to. We hadn't ever spoken about him or anyone associated with me. I said that at least we had each other's numbers and could stay in touch. I wasn't one to discuss such things – no soaps for me – but, as we texted each other, the message was that a coffee in Nero's, extra hot, was still on the agenda, however long it took.

That day did come, a Friday, about six weeks later. He'd got his mojo and his new partner back apparently. Good for him, but let's leave it there, shall we? No, I didn't want to know his name. I had never wanted to in my own situation. No point. I'd much rather talk about Dennis Potter or Placepotting.

Georgia was soon her lively herself again, just a slightly different lady in a slightly different configuration. The great news was that her Dictaphone was on for three nights at the Progress Hall in Eltham, not far from me in Lee. I said I'd be there in disguise on one of the nights but wouldn't want to make myself known or chat to the cast milling around afterwards. No thanks.

Instead, we met in Nero's on the following Monday and I told her she was very good with words and how much I loved the twist. She should stick at it and she should stick at everything else she did, that creativity was her thing, her passion. Sticking to our routine also made sense.

The best time of the year arrived, autumn, and as we had already liked to make recommendations to each other – books and films, The Hairdresser's Husband, and music – I intended to nominate October Song by The Incredible String Band, but as ever it was overtaken by a simple question from a grinning Georgia: 'Roger, tell me, how's that latest short story of yours going, and do you need a world-class proof reader?'

I told her it had gone pretty well and was very nearly finished, and was longer than the average story so far at around 4,500 words. That might be because, for the first time, I'd actually hinted at romance, which I'd avoided like Farage in the first 20 stories.

I put down what was left of the apricot croissant, and added: 'I just wanted to get across a variation on that old chestnut about friendship being more important than falling for someone with all its trials and complications.

'I struggled to get the kind of twist that most of the others had, but I think it's got a good ending.'

About the author

PETER CORDWELL was born in a Catford prefab in November, 1947. He passed the 11-plus at nearby Forster Park primary school but domeheads at Brockley County Grammar School (now defunct) turned him down after hearing that his Dad was a driver and his Mum a homehelp.

He was a journalist for more than 50 years, starting at the Kentish Independent in Woolwich and eventually becoming Sports Editor/Editor of the SE London Mercury and Greenwich Time, Greenwich Council's newspaper nicknamed 'Pravda' (and that's another story). He received two UK press awards, the second for the fans' campaign to get Charlton Athletic back to their home at The Valley.

He also played two seasons for VPS (Vaasan Palloseura) in the Finnish premier division (1975/76) and wrote the proletarian George Orwell musical/cabaret One Georgie Orwell with Charlton singer-songwriter Carl Picton.

57023493R00020